TO Vivianne and Sonja   20
 Merry Christmas
Love, Mammie + PAPA

RUDOLPH
THE
RED-NOSED REINDEER®

THE CLASSIC STORY
BASED ON THE ORIGINAL TELEVISION CLASSIC, 1964-2014

RUDOLPH
THE
RED-NOSED REINDEER®

THE CLASSIC STORY
BASED ON THE ORIGINAL TELEVISION CLASSIC, 1964-2014

RETOLD BY THEA FELDMAN

ILLUSTRATED BY ERWIN MADRID

SQUARE
FISH
NEW YORK

SQUARE
FISH

An
Imprint
of Macmillan
175 Fifth Avenue
New York, NY 10010
mackids.com

Square Fish books may be purchased for business or promotional use. For information
on bulk purchases, please contact the Macmillan Corporate and Premium Sales Department
at (800) 221-7945 x5442 or by e-mail at specialmarkets@macmillan.com.

Library of Congress Cataloging-in-Publication Data Available

ISBN: 978-1-250-04760-1 • Book design by Anna Booth

Square Fish
logo designed
by Filomena Tuosto

First Edition: 2014

10 9 8 7 6 5 4 3 2 1

RUDOLPH
THE
RED-NOSED REINDEER®

THE CLASSIC STORY
BASED ON THE ORIGINAL TELEVISION CLASSIC, 1964-2014

Way up at the North Pole, there is a special place called Christmastown. Families of reindeer live in cozy caves. Elves work at the factory, making presents for children. In Santa's castle, Mrs. Claus makes sure he eats plenty so that his holiday suit fits just right.

Everyone loves living in Christmastown. Except for one year when the weather was so bad that Christmas was almost cancelled!

One spring, Donner, the lead reindeer who helped pull Santa's sleigh each Christmas, became a proud papa. He and his wife named their son Rudolph. Soon after little Rudolph was born, his tiny red nose began to glow!

"Great bouncing icebergs!" exclaimed Santa when he saw this. If Rudolph's nose continued to glow, Santa said, he would never make the sleigh team when he grew up.

Donner taught Rudolph all the things a young reindeer needed to know—especially to beware of the Abominable Snow Monster. All the while, he hid Rudolph's nose under a cover and hoped it would someday stop glowing.

As the months went by, the elves were busy making Christmas toys. All the elves loved their work, except for one: Hermey just didn't have a knack for toy-making. Maybe that's because he dreamed of becoming a dentist one day. This made him feel like a misfit among his fellow elves.

Rudolph felt like a misfit too. He didn't like the nose cover he had to wear. Without it, his nose glowed as brightly as ever, but Donner was determined to keep that a secret.

On the day of the annual Reindeer Games, Rudolph met Clarice, a pretty young doe. When Clarice said she liked him, Rudolph was so excited that he flew through the air with joy. Flying was exactly what Comet the coach was trying to teach the young reindeer. Everyone was amazed by Rudolph—until his nose cover fell off.

All the other reindeer, except for Clarice, laughed at Rudolph and called him names. Comet said, "From now on, we won't let Rudolph join in any Reindeer Games." Rudolph went off by himself, feeling sad.

At the toy factory, Hermey was having trouble too. He skipped elf practice so he could fix dolls' teeth, thinking he might fit in better that way. When the foreman found out, he yelled, "Come to elf practice and learn to wiggle your ears and chuckle warmly and do important stuff like that. Or you'll never fit in!" But Hermey just couldn't. He ran away instead.

Before long, Hermey and Rudolph met and shared their stories. They decided to go off into the world together.

"You don't mind my red nose?" asked Rudolph.

"Not if you don't mind my being a dentist," replied Hermey.

"It's a deal!" said Rudolph.

On their first day, they heard the Abominable Snow Monster's terrible roar! "He must have seen your nose!" cried Hermey. The two friends tried to stay far ahead of the monster.

Soon, they met Yukon Cornelius and his dogsled team. Yukon was looking for gold, but he found Rudolph and Hermey instead. Then Rudolph's glowing nose let the Abominable Snow Monster find them all! Thanks to Yukon's quick thinking, they escaped on an ice floe.

The ice floe carried them to the Island of
Misfit Toys, a place filled with odd toys.

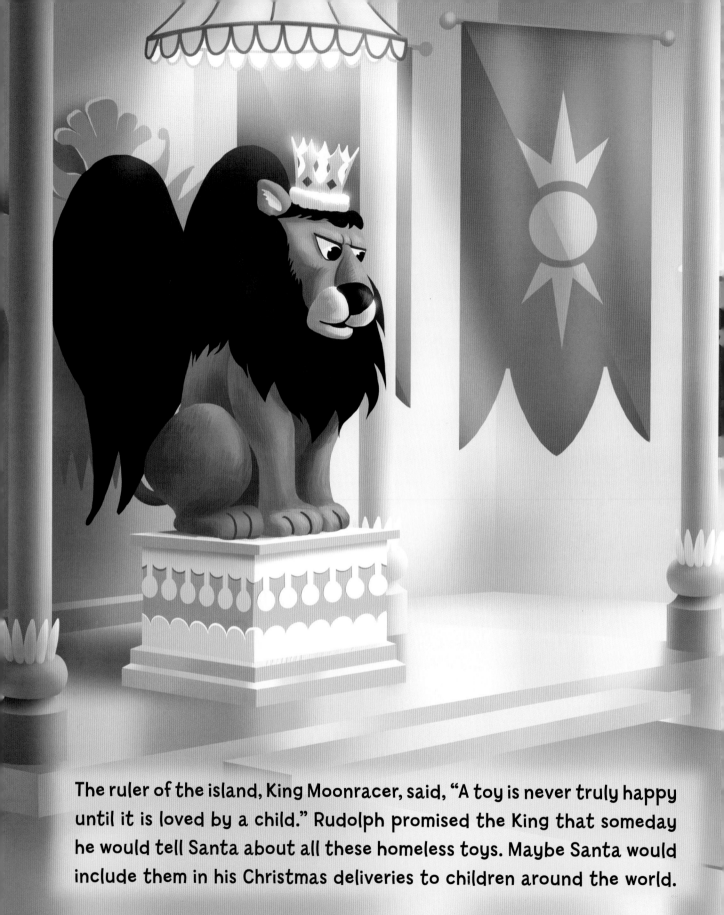

The ruler of the island, King Moonracer, said, "A toy is never truly happy until it is loved by a child." Rudolph promised the King that someday he would tell Santa about all these homeless toys. Maybe Santa would include them in his Christmas deliveries to children around the world.

Rudolph asked King Moonracer if he and his friends could stay on the Island of Misfit Toys. "This island is not for living things," said the King. "It's only for misfit toys."

"How do you like that!" said Yukon. "Even among misfits, we're misfits!"

The King let the friends rest overnight before they moved on. When Hermey and Yukon were asleep, Rudolph slipped away. Knowing that his nose would put them in constant danger with the Abominable Snow Monster, he didn't want to be the cause of any harm to his friends.

The Abominable Snow Monster did indeed find Rudolph because of his glowing nose. He chased the young reindeer everywhere. During that time, Rudolph grew up. One day, he realized it was time to go home.

Meanwhile, Rudolph's parents and Clarice had been out looking for him ever since he left. It was now two days before Christmas Eve, and Santa told Rudolph that without Donner, he'd never be able to get his sleigh off the ground.

Rudolph was determined to find his parents and Clarice. As he began to look for them, the storm of all storms hit! Thick snowflakes fell, making it hard to see.

Rudolph had an idea where his parents and Clarice were—in the cave of the Abominable Snow Monster! He made his way there despite the storm and found Clarice in the monster's clutches.

"Put her down!" Rudolph cried. The Abominable Snow Monster did—and went after Rudolph instead!

Yukon and Hermey, who had been searching for their friend, arrived at the cave just in time. Quickly, they lured the monster outside and knocked him out with a big rock.

Then Hermey removed all of the monster's teeth. Finally, Hermey got to be a dentist!

When the Abominable Snow Monster woke up, Yukon pushed him back . . . and back . . . and back . . . until the monster, Yukon, and his dogs all slipped over the edge of a cliff!

Rudolph and his friends and family were heartbroken when they returned to Christmastown. When the others heard the entire story, they realized that those who are different are important too. They all apologized to Rudolph and Hermey. The foreman even told Hermey he could open up his own dentist's office! And Santa agreed to find homes for the misfit toys.

Just then, there was a knock at the door. It was Yukon, his dogs, and the Abominable Snow Monster! Even though they had all gone over the cliff, the Abominable Snow Monster was able to bounce! And so they had all landed safely.

Now the monster was no longer mean. He even got a job: He placed the star on top of the Christmas tree. Everyone cheered!

The next day was Christmas Eve, but the weather was so bad that Santa could not fly his sleigh safely through it. He reluctantly started to tell everyone that Christmas was going to be cancelled for the first time ever. But then he realized that there was a way through the storm after all.

"Rudolph," Santa said, "you and that wonderful nose of yours—that nose can cut through the murkiest storm.

Rudolph with your nose so bright,
won't you guide my sleigh tonight?"

Rudolph replied, "It will be an honor, sir!"

The sleigh was loaded, the reindeer got into place, and Santa climbed aboard. Rudolph took the lead, and the sleigh took off. Santa's first stop? The Island of Misfit Toys. Everyone had an extra-merry Christmas that year, and Rudolph went down in history as the greatest reindeer of all time!